Blac Web

Dr. Monique Rodgers

Black Widow's Web

Dr. Monique Rodgers

United States of America

Published by Shooting Stars Publishing House 2025

ISBN:

Dedication

To the strong women who know the power of patience, strategy, and silence. To those who have been underestimated and those who never stop fighting, even when the world thinks they've already lost. This one's for you.

To the dreamers, the schemers, and the survivors—this is our story, even when it's told in shadows. May we always know when to strike and when to step back.

And to the ones who dare to play the game—may you always remember that the web you weave will either trap you... or set you free.

— Dr. Monique Rodgers

Contents

Dr. Monique Rodgers

Introduction

In a world where trust is a rare currency and power is often hidden behind a smile, Takina Burshedo reigns supreme. Known in the underground as the "Black Widow," she is a master of manipulation, seduction, and, when necessary, silence. With a mind sharper than a diamond and a carefully curated persona that leaves men craving her, Takina's reputation precedes her wherever she goes. Her weapon of choice? Trust. And when trust isn't enough, she knows how to make a quiet exit, leaving nothing but a trail of broken hearts—and sometimes, broken lives.

As we enter Takina's world, we meet her at the height of her deadly game. In the glittering world of Atlanta's elite, she's eyeing her next target: Jake Winchester, a tech bro with more money than sense. He's the perfect mark, ripe for the picking. But what happens when a game of hearts and minds takes a dangerous turn? What happens when the woman who controls every situation finds herself at a crossroads, forced to face her own tangled web of lies, secrets, and desires?

Black Widow's Web is a pulse-pounding tale of power, deception, and passion. Takina is a woman who never lets her guard down—until one night, she does. And when she does, it might just cost her everything. This is a story of seduction, betrayal, and a deadly woman who knows how to play the game—and win. Welcome to the world of Takina Burshedo, where love is just another weapon, and trust is something you should never give too freely.

Chapter 1:

Meet Takina

Takina Burshedo isn't your average woman. With a wardrobe full of sleek designer fits, an arsenal of seductive charm, and a mind sharper than a diamond cutter, she's built a reputation in the underground as a heartbreaker with a deadly twist. Her weapon of choice? Trust—and when that's not enough, a touch of poison.

We meet her at a swanky lounge in Atlanta, her favorite hunting ground. With smooth jazz playing in the background, she locks eyes with her next mark: Jake Winchester, a suave tech bro with too much money and not enough street smarts.

The dim lighting of *Euphoria Lounge* gave it that perfect mix of mystery and luxury—a playground for the rich and reckless. Takina Burshedo leaned back in her booth, the shimmering gold of her sleek Versace dress catching the flicker of candlelight. Her nails, painted a deep crimson, tapped rhythmically against her cocktail glass. She wasn't just dressed to kill—she *was* the kill, wrapped in silk and secrets.

The jazz band on stage played a sultry tune, setting the vibe for whispered deals and stolen glances. Takina's eyes scanned the room, sharp as a predator's. She wasn't here to sip overpriced martinis; she was here to hunt.

That's when she saw him.

Jake Winchester.

A classic tech bro with a face like he just walked out of a luxury watch ad. His tailored navy suit clung to his frame, the Rolex on his wrist catching every flicker of

Dr. Monique Rodgers

light. He laughed too loudly at a joke one of his buddies told, his arrogance practically oozing off him. Money had clearly come easy for Jake, and in Takina's world, that made him the perfect target.

Too much cash. Not enough brains, she thought, her lips curling into a dangerous smirk.

The Setup

Takina stood, her Louboutins clicking against the marble floor as she made her way to the bar. Every movement was calculated—hips swayed just enough to draw eyes, but her expression stayed cool, detached. Jake's gaze found her before she even reached her destination.

"Damn," he muttered to his friend, sitting up straighter. "Who's *that*?"

Takina ordered a martini, taking her time, letting him stew. When she finally turned, their eyes locked.

"You look like you're having fun," she said, her voice smooth as velvet.

Jake grinned, leaning against the bar. "I am now. What's your name?"

"Takina." She extended her hand, letting her fingers linger just long enough to send a message. "And you?"

"Jake," he replied, his eyes doing a not-so-subtle sweep of her figure. "Let me guess, you're new in town?"

She chuckled softly. "Not exactly. I just like to stay... under the radar."

Jake was hooked, his chest puffing out as he tried to impress her with stories of his startup's latest success.

Takina listened, nodding in all the right places, her mind already calculating her next move.

The Invitation

It didn't take long for Jake to suggest they head somewhere quieter.

"There's a private lounge upstairs," he offered, his hand already on the small of her back. "Way more chill than down here."

Takina gave him a coy smile. "Lead the way."

The private lounge was even more extravagant, with plush leather couches and a panoramic view of Atlanta's skyline. Jake poured them drinks, clearly feeling himself as he bragged about his penthouse, his cars, and his plans to "disrupt the tech industry."

Takina leaned in closer, her fingers brushing his arm. "You're impressive, Jake. But tell me... what's your weakness?"

Jake laughed, running a hand through his perfectly styled hair. "Weakness? I don't think I have one."

Takina's smile widened. "Everyone has one. It's just a matter of finding it."

The Strike

As the night wore on, Takina played her role to perfection—laughing at his jokes, touching his arm just enough to keep him hooked. By the time he suggested they head back to his place, Jake was practically putty in her hands.

But Takina wasn't about to waste time on pillow talk. As soon as they stepped into the elevator, she made her move.

Her hand slid up his chest, her lips brushing against his ear. "You know, Jake," she whispered, her voice low and seductive, "I think I've figured out your weakness."

Jake smirked. "Yeah? What's that?"

Without warning, Takina pressed him against the elevator wall, her knee pinning him in place. In one swift motion, she pulled a small syringe from her clutch and jabbed it into his neck.

Jake's eyes widened. "W-what the hell?" he stammered, his body already starting to go limp.

Takina stepped back, watching as he slumped to the floor.

"Arrogance," she said, crouching down beside him. "It's always arrogance."

The Cover-Up

By the time the elevator reached Jake's penthouse, he was unconscious. Takina dragged him into the living room, her movements efficient and practiced. She wasn't new to this game.

She rifled through his wallet and phone, snapping photos of his banking information and transferring a hefty sum to an untraceable account.

"You shouldn't have made it so easy," she muttered, slipping her phone back into her clutch.

Before leaving, Takina arranged the scene to look like an overdose—empty bottles of pills scattered on the coffee table, a spilled glass of whiskey by his hand. Satisfied, she smoothed her dress and stepped into the elevator.

The Exit

As she walked back into the night, the city buzzed around her, oblivious to the storm she'd just unleashed. Takina hailed a cab, slipping into the backseat with a satisfied sigh.

"Where to?" the driver asked.

"Anywhere but here," she replied, her lips curling into a smirk.

As the cab pulled away, Takina glanced at her reflection in the window. She wasn't just a

Dr. Monique Rodgers

woman—she was a force of nature, unstoppable and untouchable.

And Jake Winchester? Just another name on her growing list of conquests.

Chapter 2:

Love Bombing and Luxury

Takina plays her role flawlessly—sweet, sassy, and just vulnerable enough to make Jake feel like he's got the upper hand. They sip on top-shelf whiskey as she listens intently to his dreams of "changing the world" through some startup app. Inside, she's rolling her eyes. Outwardly, she's all dimples and giggles.

Jake falls fast, inviting her into his luxurious life of private jets, yacht parties, and opulent mansions. Takina soaks it all in, plotting her next move.

The warm glow of the penthouse candles made everything look like it was dipped in gold, but Takina knew better. The luxury surrounding her wasn't hers—not yet. Perched on a sleek leather couch, she held a crystal glass of whiskey in one hand, swirling

Dr. Monique Rodgers

the amber liquid like she actually cared about tasting it. Across from her, Jake Winchester leaned forward, gesturing wildly as he talked about his new app.

"I'm telling you, Takina," he said, his voice full of that tech-bro confidence, "this isn't just an app—it's a revolution. We're talking global impact, real-world change, disrupting the market entirely."

Disrupting the market? Boy, you just rebranded grocery delivery, she thought, hiding her smirk behind a sip of whiskey. Instead, she giggled, letting her dimples do the work.

"That's incredible, Jake," she said, her voice soft but supportive. "You must be, like, crazy smart to come up with something so... big."

Jake grinned, leaning back like he'd just won an award. "It's not just smarts, babe. It's vision. You have to see things other people don't."

"Oh, I see things alright," she murmured under her breath, still smiling sweetly.

The Sweet Trap

Takina knew how to play the game. She tilted her head just so, making her earrings catch the light, and let out a small laugh every time Jake cracked a lame joke. She threw in just enough vulnerability—mentioning a rough childhood, a dream she'd never chased—to make him think he was unlocking her heart.

"You know," she said, staring at the skyline through the massive floor-to-ceiling windows, "I've never really had anyone believe in me before. Not the way you talk about your team."

Jake's brow furrowed, his knight-in-shining-armor instincts kicking in. "What? That's insane. You're incredible, Takina. Anyone who can't see that is blind."

She looked down, biting her lip as if she was holding back tears. Inside, she was laughing. *Hook, line, sinker.*

"You're sweet," she whispered, her voice trembling just enough to sell the act. "I just... I don't want to get in your way. You've got this whole empire you're building, and I'm just..."

"You're not 'just' anything," Jake interrupted, moving closer. He grabbed her hand, squeezing it like he was swearing some unspoken oath. "You're special, Takina. And I want you to be part of this. Part of everything."

High-Life Love Bombing

The next few weeks were a blur of opulence. Jake was relentless with his lovebombing—sending Takina flowers so massive they barely fit through her apartment door, texting her good morning and goodnight like clockwork, and whisking her away on spontaneous adventures.

There was the private jet ride to Miami for a "networking event" that turned into an all-night yacht party. Takina dazzled in a custom gown Jake had "insisted" on buying, sipping champagne as she watched the city lights dance on the water.

"You look like you belong here," Jake said, wrapping an arm around her waist.

"Maybe I do," she teased, leaning into him.

The Setup

By the time Jake took her to his Hamptons mansion, Takina had mapped out his entire routine. She knew which safe held his rarest watches, which drawer had his passwords scribbled on a notepad, and which nights he stayed up late working in his home office.

"This place is... wow," Takina said, letting her fingers trail along the marble countertops.

Jake grinned, standing behind her and wrapping his arms around her waist. "You like it? It's yours too, you know. All of this. I want to share it with you."

Takina turned, her hands resting on his chest. "You don't have to say stuff like that, Jake."

"I'm serious," he said, brushing a strand of hair from her face. "You're different. I've never felt this way before."

Plotting the Move

Later that night, while Jake slept soundly in their massive four-poster bed, Takina slipped into the living room. She poured herself a glass of wine, her mind racing as she pieced everything together.

This dude really thinks I'm his soulmate, she thought, shaking her head. *Poor baby. Doesn't even realize he's the next chapter in my book.*

She opened his laptop, typing in the password she'd seen him enter earlier that day. The screen lit up with his financial dashboard—a goldmine of accounts and investments.

She sipped her wine, her fingers hovering over the keyboard. "Not yet," she whispered to herself. "Soon, though."

The Closer

The next morning, Jake woke to the smell of fresh coffee and bacon. Takina stood in the kitchen wearing one of his oversized shirts, humming along to a playlist she'd found on his phone.

"This is new," he said, wrapping his arms around her from behind.

"I just wanted to do something nice for you," she said, turning her head to kiss his cheek. "You've been so amazing, Jake. I don't even know how to thank you."

Jake grinned, spinning her around to face him. "Just stay, Takina. That's all I want."

Her heart-shaped lips curved into a smile as she gazed up at him. "I'll stay," she said softly, pressing her lips to his.

Inwardly, though, she was already counting the days.

Time to plan my exit. And Jake? You're footing the bill.

Chapter 3:

Secrets in the Shadows

The candlelight flickered in the massive dining room, casting shadows on the high walls. Takina sat across from Jake at the sleek, polished table, her eyes shimmering with the kind of vulnerability she had spent years perfecting. She swirled the wine in her glass, staring into the deep red liquid as if it held some secret she was reluctant to share.

"You ever think about where you come from?" she asked suddenly, breaking the comfortable silence.

Jake looked up from his steak, his brow furrowed. "Where's this coming from?"

Takina shrugged, the movement casual, but her tone carried a weight that drew him in. "Just... thinking

Dr. Monique Rodgers

about how different my life would've been if I had half the chances you had."

"You don't give yourself enough credit," Jake said, reaching across the table to take her hand. "You're brilliant, Takina. You've made it here, with me. That says something."

A small, almost imperceptible smile played on her lips. *Hooked.* "Yeah, but my roots? They weren't pretty, Jake. My dad? He walked out when I was six. My mom? Worked three jobs to keep a roof over our heads. I learned real young that you can't trust anyone to stick around."

Jake's grip on her hand tightened slightly, and she could see the sympathy pooling in his eyes. "That's tough. I'm sorry you had to go through that."

She let out a small, bitter laugh, pulling her hand back to tuck a strand of hair behind her ear. "It is what it is. Made me who I am. But sometimes... I wish I didn't have to be so strong, you know? Like, it'd be nice to let someone else carry the weight for once."

Jake leaned forward, his voice low and earnest. "You don't have to carry it alone anymore. You've got me now."

The Deflection Game

Jake's words hung in the air, heavy with sincerity, but Takina's smile faltered for a fraction of a second before she plastered it back on. She sipped her wine, letting the silence linger just long enough to shift the dynamic.

"You're sweet, Jake," she said softly. "But let's not get too deep. I don't wanna ruin the mood."

Jake chuckled, leaning back in his chair. "Alright, we'll keep it light. But you're an open book to me, Takina. Anything you want to share, I'm here."

She tilted her head, her eyes narrowing playfully. "Careful, Mr. Winchester. You don't want to know all my secrets."

"Try me," he said, grinning.

Takina's laugh was light, almost musical, but there was a glint in her eyes that betrayed her amusement. *You couldn't handle half of them, babe.* Instead of answering, she stood, rounding the table to perch on his lap. She ran a manicured finger down his chest, shifting the conversation entirely.

"So, what's your biggest secret?" she asked, her voice low and teasing.

Jake smirked, his hands settling on her hips. "You first."

"Ladies don't spill their tea so easily," she quipped, leaning down to brush her lips against his ear. "But maybe I can distract you from asking too many questions."

A Dangerous Distraction

The tension between them snapped like a taut string, and Jake pulled her closer, their mouths colliding in a heated kiss. Takina's hands tangled in his hair as he lifted her effortlessly, carrying her to the expansive couch in the living room.

Dr. Monique Rodgers

The soft glow from the fireplace bathed them in a golden hue as they shed their layers. Jake's hands explored her curves, his touch reverent yet hungry. Takina responded with equal fervor, her lips tracing a line down his jaw as she whispered his name like a prayer.

"This is what I need," she murmured against his skin. "Someone who sees me."

"I see you, Takina," he whispered back, his voice thick with emotion.

No, you see what I want you to see, she thought, but she moaned softly instead, letting him believe he was the hero in her story.

Unraveling the Past

Later, as they lay entwined on the couch, Jake traced lazy circles on her bare shoulder. The air between them felt charged, as if the intimacy had brought them closer—but not close enough for Takina to let her guard down.

"Tell me about your ex-fiancé," Jake said suddenly, his voice soft but probing.

Takina stiffened for a fraction of a second before letting out a shaky breath. "Why do you want to know about him?"

"Because I want to know you," Jake said simply. "The real you."

She sat up, pulling the blanket around her shoulders like a shield. "He wasn't what I thought he was, okay? I trusted him, and he... let's just say he didn't deserve it."

Jake frowned, concern etched on his face. "What happened?"

Takina hesitated, then gave a half-truth. "He cheated. Lied to me. Made me feel like I wasn't enough."

Jake pulled her into his arms, his grip protective. "You're more than enough, Takina. That guy was an idiot."

She buried her face in his chest, letting herself relax against him. "Thanks, Jake," she murmured, her voice muffled. "You're different. I don't know what I'd do if I lost you."

Jake held her tighter, unaware of the storm brewing beneath her calm exterior. Takina's mind raced, calculating her next move. She'd given him just enough to keep him invested, to make him feel like he was peeling back her layers. But the truth? The truth would bury him—and she wasn't ready to let go of her golden ticket just yet.

Not until the game's over.

Chapter 4:

The Turning Point

The private jet touched down on Aspen's snow-blanketed runway, the evening sky painted with streaks of pink and orange. Takina stepped onto the tarmac in a sleek faux fur coat, her diamond earrings catching the fading sunlight. She flashed Jake a dazzling smile as he helped her down the steps.

"Snow bunnies are about to be *jealous*," she teased, brushing a perfectly manicured nail against his tailored coat. "You sure know how to spoil a girl, Mr. Winchester."

Jake smirked, wrapping an arm around her waist. "Nothing but the best for my queen. Wait until you see what I've got planned."

The cabin they arrived at was a luxurious masterpiece nestled in the mountains, its floor-to-ceiling windows offering breathtaking views of the Rockies. Inside, the warmth of the crackling fireplace contrasted with the crisp air outside. Takina took it all in, her mind already working overtime.

The Proposal

Dinner was served on a glass table adorned with rose petals and flickering candles. Takina sipped on Dom Pérignon, the bubbles tickling her throat as Jake fidgeted nervously across from her.

"You okay, babe?" she asked, her brow arched in playful curiosity.

"Yeah, yeah, I'm good," he replied, though his hand trembled slightly as he set down his glass.

Before she could press him, he stood, reaching into his pocket. Takina's heart skipped a beat—not from anticipation but from calculation. She already knew what was coming.

"Takina," Jake began, his voice steady despite the nerves written across his face. He dropped to one knee, holding up a velvet box that opened to reveal a massive, sparkling diamond ring.

"Oh my God," Takina gasped, one hand flying to her chest. *He's really doing this.*

"You've changed my life in ways I didn't think were possible," Jake said, his tone sincere. "You make me better, stronger... happier. I don't want to imagine a life without you in it. Will you marry me?"

Takina let the pause hang in the air, milking the moment as she calculated her response. Finally, she smiled, her eyes glistening with crocodile tears.

"Yes, Jake," she whispered, her voice quivering just enough. "Yes, I'll marry you."

As Jake slipped the ring onto her finger, Takina leaned in, her lips brushing against his in a kiss that was equal parts tender and possessive. But behind her smile, her mind raced. *Time to start planning my exit strategy.*

The Prenup Bombshell

Back in Atlanta, the honeymoon glow of their engagement was quickly dimmed by reality. Takina lounged on the plush couch of Jake's penthouse, flipping through wedding magazines when he walked in with a manila folder.

Dr. Monique Rodgers

"What's that?" she asked, not looking up.

Jake hesitated before sitting beside her. "It's... uh... something we should talk about."

Takina set the magazine down, her perfectly arched brows knitting together. "What's up?"

Jake handed her the folder, avoiding eye contact. "It's a prenup. Just a formality, you know? To protect both of us."

The smile on Takina's face froze, and for a split second, her mask cracked. "A prenup?" she repeated, her voice laced with hurt.

"It's nothing personal," Jake said quickly, sensing her shift in mood. "I just—my lawyers insisted. You know how it is."

"Do I?" Takina asked, her tone icy now. She stood, the folder clutched tightly in her hand. "Because what it sounds like is you don't trust me."

Jake sighed, running a hand through his hair. "Baby, it's not about trust. It's about being smart. This doesn't change how I feel about you."

"Oh, it doesn't?" she shot back, her eyes narrowing. "Because it feels like you're already planning for us to fail."

Jake reached for her, but she stepped back. "Takina, come on. Don't do this."

She laughed bitterly, shaking her head. "You're unbelievable, Jake. You ask me to be your wife, to build a life with you, and then you hit me with *this*?!"

Her voice cracked on the last word, and Jake softened, standing to pull her into his arms. She didn't resist, though her mind seethed.

"I love you," he murmured into her hair. "This doesn't mean I don't believe in us. It's just... business."

Takina pulled back slightly, her face tilted up toward his. "Business," she echoed, her tone softer now. "Fine. I'll sign it. But just so you know, Jake, love isn't a business. And if you don't figure that out, this marriage is doomed before it even starts."

A Dangerous Passion

Later that night, the tension melted away as Jake and Takina found themselves tangled in each other. The city lights outside cast long shadows across the room as Jake kissed a fiery trail down her neck.

Dr. Monique Rodgers

"I don't deserve you," he whispered, his breath hot against her skin.

"No," Takina replied, threading her fingers through his hair. "You don't."

Her words carried a double meaning, but Jake was too lost in her to notice. Their movements were desperate, almost frantic, as if trying to erase the lingering doubt that had crept between them.

As Jake's hands roamed her body, Takina let herself get lost in the moment, knowing that this passion was as fleeting as a shooting star. Her mind was already on the next step, but for now, she let herself play the role of the devoted fiancée.

"Promise me something," Jake murmured as they lay tangled together afterward.

"What?" Takina asked, tracing circles on his chest.

"No more secrets," he said, his voice heavy with meaning.

Takina smiled, leaning up to kiss him softly. "No more secrets," she echoed.

But as Jake drifted off to sleep, Takina stared at the ceiling, her thoughts a whirlwind of plans and possibilities. The clock was ticking, and her exit strategy was already in motion.

Chapter 5:

Poison in the Champagne

The penthouse gleamed under the city lights, the kind of place you'd expect a power couple to spend their nights. Takina had set the stage: soft jazz played low, candles flickered on the marble dining table, and the aroma of her "homemade" steak dinner—courtesy of a private chef—wafted through the room. She glanced at the bottle of Cristal chilling in its silver bucket. Everything was perfect.

Jake walked in from the balcony, his sleeves rolled up and tie loosened. "Damn, babe, you went all out," he said, grinning as he adjusted his Rolex.

She flashed him her killer smile. "You only live once, right?" *Literally*, she thought to herself.

Jake approached the table, pulling her close by the waist. "You spoil me, you know that?"

"Only because you deserve it," she purred, her lips brushing his ear. Her fingers trailed down his arm as she stepped away to grab the champagne.

The Setup

Takina popped the cork with a practiced ease, pouring two glasses with a grace that could've landed her in a luxury ad. Her movements were smooth, deliberate. From her pocket, she palmed a tiny vial, twisting off the cap with one hand.

She turned her back to Jake for just a second, pretending to adjust her bracelet as she tipped the poison into his glass. The liquid dissolved instantly, invisible, undetectable.

"Perfect pour," she said, spinning around and handing him the glass.

Jake raised an eyebrow. "To us?"

"To forever," she replied, her voice like silk.

The Toast

They clinked glasses, the sound ringing out like a death knell. Jake took a generous sip, his eyes locked on hers. "You're somethin' else, Takina," he said, leaning back in his chair.

"I'll take that as a compliment," she replied, swirling the champagne in her glass but not drinking.

Jake tilted his head. "You're not drinking?"

She laughed lightly, feigning surprise. "Of course I am," she said, taking the tiniest sip. "Just savoring it."

Dr. Monique Rodgers

The Tension Rises

Dinner continued, Jake oblivious as Takina's smile grew sharper with every bite he took, every sip he swallowed. Her heart beat steadily, her nerves honed to perfection. She'd done this before. But Jake... he was different.

"So, what's next for us?" Jake asked, cutting into his steak.

"Next?" Takina repeated, tilting her head as if pondering. "I was thinking maybe Europe for the honeymoon. Paris, Venice, Santorini—something classic."

Jake chuckled. "You've already got it planned, huh?"

"Always thinking ahead," she said smoothly. *Way ahead.*

The Moment

Dr. Monique Rodgers

Jake set his fork down, a hand going to his chest. "Weird," he muttered. "Feel a little off."

Takina's eyes narrowed slightly. "Off? How?" she asked, her voice calm, curious.

"Dunno," he said, leaning back in his chair. "Just... dizzy. Maybe it's the champagne."

She leaned forward, her expression concerned but not too concerned. "You okay, babe? Want me to call someone?"

Jake waved her off. "Nah, I'm good. Probably just tired or somethin'."

But as the seconds ticked by, his breathing grew heavier, his movements sluggish. "This... this ain't right," he said, his voice slurring.

Takina stood, her chair scraping against the floor. "Jake? What's going on?" she asked, her tone laced with faux worry.

"I—" His words cut off as he doubled over, clutching his stomach.

The Kill

Jake collapsed onto the floor, gasping for air as his body convulsed. Takina crouched beside him, brushing a hand through his hair.

"Shhh, it's okay," she whispered, her voice soft, almost tender. "You're just feeling the consequences of your own choices."

He looked up at her, his eyes wide with confusion and betrayal. "W-why?" he choked out.

Takina tilted her head, her expression devoid of remorse. "Should've read the fine print, babe."

Jake's body went still, his final breath escaping in a shallow rasp. Takina stood, smoothing her dress as she looked down at him.

The Cover-Up

Without missing a beat, Takina grabbed her phone, dialing a burner number. "It's done," she said simply.

"Need cleanup?" a gravelly voice on the other end asked.

"Obviously," she replied, rolling her eyes as she stepped over Jake's body. "Same rate as usual."

"Got it. ETA twenty."

Dr. Monique Rodgers

She ended the call, tossing the phone into a drawer. She adjusted her hair in the mirror, her reflection calm and composed. Then she grabbed her glass of untouched champagne, raising it in a silent toast to herself.

"Here's to forever," she said, smirking as she took a victorious sip.

Chapter 6:

Cleaning Up the Mess

The penthouse was eerily quiet now, save for the faint hum of the city outside. Takina stood over Jake's lifeless body, her expression unreadable. She pulled off her diamond earrings, setting them neatly on the counter, and rolled up the sleeves of her silk blouse. If there was one thing she knew how to do, it was cleaning up a mess.

Step One: Erase the Evidence

She grabbed her kit from the hall closet—a designer bag filled with rubber gloves, bleach wipes, and everything else she needed to vanish without a trace. Sliding on a pair of gloves, she moved with precision, wiping down the champagne flutes, the bottle, and the silverware Jake had used.

"No fingerprints, no problems," she muttered under her breath, her voice steady.

She crouched by Jake's body, checking his pockets for anything incriminating—his phone, wallet, and the ring box she'd seen him tuck away earlier. She smirked as she pocketed the ring. "Guess you won't need this anymore, babe."

She worked quickly, wiping down the chair he'd been sitting in, the table, even the edge of the counter he might've leaned on. Every move was calculated, rehearsed.

Step Two: Play the Role

Once the scene was spotless, Takina swapped her gloves for a new pair and pulled out her burner phone. She dialed 911, her voice trembling as she spoke.

"Please, help! My fiancé—he's not breathing!" she cried, adding a sob for dramatic effect. "We were having dinner, and he just—collapsed. Please, hurry!"

The dispatcher assured her help was on the way. Takina hung up, tossing the burner into the trash compactor and pressing the button. She watched as the device was crushed into oblivion.

Step Three: Prepare the Performance

She ran to the bathroom, splashing water on her face to make her eyes red and puffy. Pulling a tissue from the box, she dabbed at her cheeks, practicing her panicked expression in the mirror.

"Perfect," she whispered, nodding at her reflection.

She grabbed Jake's phone, unlocking it with his thumb, and sent a quick text to his assistant. *Feeling off—might call it an early night.* It was subtle, just enough to establish a timeline.

The Arrival

The sound of sirens echoed through the streets below. Takina rushed back to the dining room, kneeling beside Jake's body as tears streamed down her face. When the EMTs burst through the door, she was ready.

"Oh my God, please, do something!" she screamed, clutching his hand as if willing him to come back.

The paramedics worked quickly, but she knew it was useless. Still, she maintained the act, crying harder when they shook their heads.

"I don't understand," she sobbed, looking up at one of them. "We were just having dinner. He said he felt dizzy, and then he—he just—"

The Detective

An hour later, a detective arrived. Detective Harris was sharp, his eyes scanning the room like a hawk. Takina's heart rate picked up, but she kept her composure.

"Miss Burshedo, I'm sorry for your loss," Harris began, pulling out a notebook. "Mind if I ask you a few questions?"

"Of course," she sniffled, dabbing at her nose.

He tilted his head. "When did Mr. Winchester start feeling unwell?"

"Right after we toasted," she said, her voice breaking. "He said he felt dizzy, but I thought maybe it was just the champagne. I—I didn't think it was serious."

"And the food? Did you cook it yourself?"

She shook her head. "No, Jake insisted on having it catered. He said I deserved a night off."

Harris nodded, jotting down notes. "And the champagne?"

"It was Jake's favorite. We always keep a bottle on hand for special occasions," she replied smoothly.

The Exit Strategy

Harris asked a few more questions, but Takina's answers were airtight. When he finally closed his notebook, she let out a shaky breath.

Black Widow's Web

Dr. Monique Rodgers

"Thank you for your cooperation, Miss Burshedo," he said, giving her a small nod.

"Anything to help," she murmured, clutching a tissue in her hand.

As soon as he left, Takina's tears dried up. She leaned against the counter, her mind already working through her next moves. She'd lay low for a while, let the investigation run its course. By the time they figured out the truth—if they ever did—she'd be long gone.

The Final Touch

Before leaving the penthouse, Takina slipped on her coat, grabbing Jake's watch from the counter. She admired it for a moment before sliding it onto her wrist.

"Thanks for everything, Jake," she whispered, her lips curling into a smirk.

As she stepped into the elevator, the city stretched out before her, glittering and alive. Takina smiled to herself, already thinking about her next move.

For Takina Burshedo, this wasn't an ending. It was just another chapter in her perfectly orchestrated story.

Chapter 7:

The Investigation

The cool Atlanta night was alive with energy—cars buzzing past, neon lights reflecting off slick pavement, and music thumping from a nearby club. Takina leaned against the balcony of her midtown apartment, scrolling through her phone with one hand while the other nursed a glass of wine. The city was her playground, and tonight, she was setting the stage for her next move.

Her phone buzzed. A message from her "bestie" Alyssa, who knew her as nothing more than a bougie socialite:

Alyssa: "Girl, you coming through tonight? VIP's poppin'!"

Takina: "Maybe later. Handling some biz right now
●."

She smirked, sliding her phone into her pocket. Her current business had nothing to do with bottle service and everything to do with staying one step ahead.

The Uninvited Guest

A knock at the door startled her. She wasn't expecting anyone. Her instincts kicked in, sharp and calculating. Takina set her glass down and checked the peephole.

Detective Harris.

Her heart skipped, but she plastered on a confused smile, unlocking the door. "Detective Harris," she said, tilting her head. "This is... unexpected. What brings you here so late?"

"Evening, Miss Burshedo," Harris replied, his tone friendly but firm. "Mind if I come in? Just had a couple more questions about Jake's passing."

She hesitated for half a beat, then stepped aside. "Of course. Anything to help."

Harris walked in, his eyes scanning the room like a hawk spotting prey. Takina mentally cursed herself

for not tidying up the half-empty bottle of wine and
the takeout container on the coffee table.

"Nice place," he said casually, but there was an edge to
his voice.

"Thanks. Jake... he loved decorating," she said, her
voice wavering just enough to sell her grief.

The Interrogation

Harris wasted no time. "So, I've been digging into
Jake's life. Seems like he was a pretty private guy.

Didn't keep many close friends, no family in town. That must've made you two even closer."

She nodded, perching on the armrest of the couch. "He was my world. I still can't believe he's gone."

Harris studied her, his face unreadable. "It's funny. I talked to the catering company that handled your dinner that night. They said Jake insisted on a full staff, but then canceled last minute. Did he say why?"

Takina's stomach flipped, but her face remained a mask of confusion. "I... I didn't know he canceled. He just told me it was going to be an intimate evening."

Dr. Monique Rodgers

"Interesting," Harris said, tapping his notebook. "One more thing—did Jake ever mention any health issues? Allergies, conditions, anything like that?"

"No," she said firmly. "He was healthy as a horse."

Harris nodded slowly, his gaze narrowing. "Strange, then, how a guy like that just drops dead over dinner."

The Power Play

Takina stood, crossing her arms as if trying to hold herself together. "Detective, are you trying to imply something? Because I've been nothing but cooperative."

Harris shrugged, leaning back in his chair. "Just doing my job, ma'am. Sometimes things don't add up, and I have to ask tough questions. Like, why would someone as savvy as Jake not notice something was off with his champagne?"

Takina's pulse raced, but she kept her voice steady. "I don't know what you're getting at, but I loved Jake. If you're here to accuse me of something, maybe you should leave."

Harris stood, sliding his notebook back into his pocket. "Relax, Miss Burshedo. I'm just following up. You have a good night."

She followed him to the door, her mind racing. As he stepped out, he turned back. "Oh, one last thing. You ever been to Venice?"

Takina blinked, caught off guard. "What? No. Why?"

He smiled faintly. "Jake's credit card statement says otherwise. Guess I'll let you know if I find anything interesting."

The Aftermath

Takina locked the door, leaning against it as a cold wave of panic washed over her. Harris was digging too deep. That Venice trip had been with her last mark—a banker whose "accident" was still under investigation.

Her phone buzzed again. This time, it was a message from a burner number:

Unknown: "You slipping, T. Handle it or I will."

Her jaw tightened. She couldn't afford mistakes, and she damn sure couldn't afford loose ends.

She downed the rest of her wine, her mind already forming a plan. If Harris wanted to play detective, she'd give him a distraction he wouldn't see coming.

Setting the Stage

The next morning, Takina was all smiles as she strolled into a café downtown. She ordered a latte, paid in cash, and slid a flash drive into the payphone booth outside. A coded email was sent moments later.

That night, an anonymous tip would lead Harris to a warehouse full of counterfeit cash and a supposed "lead" on Jake's death. By the time he realized it was a setup, Takina would be miles ahead.

"Game on," she whispered, slipping into the night.

Chapter 8:

On to the Next

As the heat dies down, Takina packs up her life and moves to Miami, where she's already eyeing her next target—a wealthy hotel mogul with a weakness for beautiful women.

She reflects on her past for a fleeting moment, not with guilt, but with pride. Every man she's taken down deserved it in her eyes—liars, cheaters, manipulators. She's not just a killer; she's a vigilante in her own twisted mind.

Takina sits on a balcony overlooking the Miami skyline, sipping on a mojito. Her phone buzzes—a text from her new mark. She smirks, already spinning her next web.

Dr. Monique Rodgers

As the sun sets, casting a fiery glow over the city, Takina leans back and whispers to herself: "Another day, another dollar."

Takina arrived in Miami, her red dress shimmering like a flame against the neon lights of South Beach. The air was thick with salt and opportunity as she stepped into *La Luxura*, an exclusive club where the city's elite came to play. Her next target, hotel mogul Victor Cruz, was holding court in the VIP section, surrounded by sycophants and champagne bottles.

"Showtime," Takina whispered, adjusting her diamond earrings.

As she glided through the club, heads turned. Men stared, women whispered. Victor noticed her instantly. His gaze lingered, a mix of curiosity and lust. She approached the bar and ordered a martini, her movements slow and deliberate, knowing he was watching.

"Make that two," Victor said, stepping beside her.

She turned, feigning surprise. "Oh, I didn't see you there."

Victor smiled, his confidence radiating. "Hard to believe. I'm usually the loudest guy in the room."

Takina tilted her head, studying him. "I'm not impressed by noise. Actions speak louder."

His grin widened. "Then let me show you what I can do."

The Seduction

Within hours, Takina was in Victor's private suite, a sprawling penthouse overlooking the ocean. He

Dr. Monique Rodgers

poured her a glass of wine, leaning in close as the city sparkled below.

"You're different," he said, brushing a strand of hair from her face. "Most women throw themselves at me, but you... you make me work for it."

Takina laughed softly. "Maybe I like seeing men sweat."

Their lips met in a fiery kiss, and Victor pulled her onto the plush couch. Takina let herself sink into the moment, her hands tracing the muscles of his back. But as his grip tightened, a flicker of her true purpose returned.

"Not yet," she whispered, pulling back with a coy smile. "I like to take my time."

Victor groaned, running a hand through his hair. "You're killing me, Takina."

Not yet, she thought. *But soon.*

The Heist Unfolds

As Victor slept, Takina slipped out of bed, her black lace robe trailing behind her. She opened his laptop, quickly bypassing his security with a USB drive loaded with spyware. His bank accounts, offshore holdings, and confidential files appeared on the screen.

"Gotcha," she murmured.

But just as she was about to finish, Victor stirred.

"Takina?" he mumbled, his voice groggy.

She closed the laptop and turned, her expression innocent. "Couldn't sleep. Your view is too distracting."

Victor smiled sleepily, pulling her back to bed. "Come here, troublemaker."

She slid under the sheets, her heart racing. *One more day,* she thought. *Then he's done.*

Chapter 9:

The Betrayal

The next evening, Takina and Victor attended a gala at one of his luxury hotels. She wore a floor-length emerald gown that clung to her curves, drawing envious glances and whispered admiration.

Victor introduced her to investors and celebrities, proudly keeping her by his side. But as the night wore on, Takina's plan hit a snag.

A woman approached—a stunning blonde with icy blue eyes and a tight smile.

"Victor," she purred, placing a hand on his arm. "Aren't you going to introduce me to your date?"

Victor stiffened. "Sophia, this isn't the time."

Sophia ignored him, focusing on Takina. "I'm his fiancée."

Takina's stomach twisted, but she didn't let it show. "Fiancée? That's... surprising."

Victor stepped between them. "Sophia, enough. We're done."

Sophia glared at him, then turned to Takina. "He's a liar. Whatever he's told you, it's a lie. You're just another game to him."

Takina met her gaze with icy calm. "Thanks for the heads-up. But I can handle myself."

Victor grabbed her arm. "Let's go."

Confrontation

Back at the penthouse, Victor tried to explain.

Dr. Monique Rodgers

"She's lying," he insisted. "We've been over for months."

Takina crossed her arms, her voice cold. "And you didn't think to mention her?"

"I didn't want to scare you off," he admitted, running a hand through his hair.

She stepped closer, her eyes blazing. "You're scared now, aren't you? Scared I'll walk away?"

Victor reached for her, but she stepped back.

"I need some air," she said, grabbing her clutch.

The next morning, Victor woke to find Takina gone. His laptop and safe had been emptied, and a single note sat on his pillow:

"Never underestimate a woman with a plan."

Chapter 10:

The Takeover

The airport buzzed with the hum of announcements and the shuffle of travelers. Takina sat in the lounge, sipping her coffee while discreetly observing her surroundings. She spotted them before they saw her—Victor's security team, clad in tailored suits, their eyes scanning the terminal like hawks.

"Damn it," she muttered, lowering her cap. Her heart thumped as she casually gathered her things and slipped toward the restrooms.

Inside, she moved with precision, swapping her sleek designer outfit for a hoodie and jeans she'd stashed in her carry-on. She tucked her hair under a baseball cap, smudged her makeup, and slipped on a pair of glasses. The woman who emerged was unrecognizable.

Sliding out through a side exit, she flagged down a cab. "Take me to the nearest hotel," she ordered, her voice steady despite the adrenaline coursing through her veins.

Her phone buzzed, a text from an unknown number: *"Nice try. We'll find you."*

Takina smirked, deleting the message. "Not if I find you first," she whispered to herself.

The Setup

At the hotel, Takina booked a room under a fake name and paid in cash. The walls felt like they were closing in, but she couldn't afford to stay put for long. She scanned her bag, ensuring her tools were ready: burner phones, cash, a taser, and a small pistol.

Her laptop pinged with an encrypted message.

Unknown Sender: *"Victor's got eyes everywhere. Tonight's your last chance to move. Coordinates attached."*

The location was an abandoned warehouse on the outskirts of the city. Takina knew it was a trap, but she also knew Victor underestimated her.

Climactic Showdown

Hours later, Takina rolled up to the warehouse on a sleek black motorcycle she'd "borrowed" from the hotel's valet. The building loomed ahead, its windows shattered and walls covered in graffiti. The scene was quiet—too quiet.

She killed the engine and stepped off, her boots crunching against the gravel. The moment she entered, the lights flickered on, illuminating Victor Cruz and his entourage.

"Takina," Victor greeted, his tone smooth but menacing. "You've been quite the headache."

"Funny," she shot back, her voice dripping with sarcasm. "I was about to say the same about you."

Victor smirked. "This doesn't have to get messy. Hand over the drive, and maybe I'll let you walk out of here."

Takina tilted her head, feigning consideration. "Tempting. But see, I've got a different ending in mind."

Without warning, she hurled a smoke bomb from her pocket, filling the room with a dense cloud. Chaos erupted as Victor's men shouted and stumbled in the haze.

Gunfire echoed as Takina moved like a shadow, taking down one guard with a swift kick and disarming another with a well-aimed punch. Her movements were fluid, lethal, and calculated.

Victor's voice cut through the commotion. "Find her!"

Takina ducked behind a pillar, catching her breath. She glanced at the exit but knew she couldn't leave without finishing this.

The Final Confrontation

When the smoke cleared, Victor stood in the center of the room, a gun in hand. "Enough games, Takina. You've always been good, but you're outnumbered."

She stepped into the open, her pistol trained on him. "Maybe. But I only need one bullet for you."

They circled each other like predators, the tension crackling in the air.

"Why, Takina?" Victor asked, his voice softer now. "We could've been unstoppable together."

Her laugh was cold. "Unstoppable? You mean under your thumb? No thanks. I'd rather burn it all down."

Victor lunged, but Takina was ready. Their fight was brutal—fists, knees, and elbows colliding in a deadly dance. She finally got the upper hand, pinning him to the ground.

"This is for all the people you've hurt," she hissed, raising her pistol.

The Escape

Takina didn't pull the trigger. Instead, she leaned in close, whispering something into Victor's ear that made his face pale. She stood and left him alive but broken, his empire crumbling in her wake.

The sound of sirens grew louder as she sped away on her motorcycle, the city lights blurring around her. She didn't look back—she never did.

Her phone buzzed again.

Unknown Number: *"You did it. Time to disappear."*

Takina smiled, the adrenaline fading into a sense of triumph. For the first time in years, she felt free.

Chapter 11:

The Ties That Bind

The city lights blinked like a thousand broken promises as Takina Burshedo watched from her penthouse window, the glow casting long shadows on her face. She could feel the weight of the world pressing against her chest, but she wasn't about to crack—not now, not ever. She had played this game too long, too well.

The phone buzzed in her pocket, breaking her from her thoughts. It was a text from an unknown number.

"We know what you did. You can't run forever."

Dr. Monique Rodgers

Takina smirked, tucking her phone back into her bag.

She wasn't scared—no, not even close. She was **too**

smart for this, and her plans were always two steps

ahead of anyone who dared to challenge her.

Tonight was supposed to be her night of reflection.

After everything that had happened, she thought she

deserved a break—a little time to recharge before the

next chapter of her carefully curated life. But she

couldn't ignore the reality: she was never truly safe.

There was always someone lurking in the shadows,

ready to pull the trigger.

She slid into her seat at the exclusive rooftop lounge,

where the music thumped in the background, mixing

with the laughter of the city's elite. Takina loved the

sound of power. It was intoxicating, like a fine wine. She was used to this world now. **She owned it.**

But tonight? Tonight was different. The tension in the air was thick enough to cut with a knife. She couldn't shake the feeling that her carefully built empire was teetering on the edge.

Her mind was running through all the scenarios—who knew? Who had connected the dots? Was it Victor's men? Or was it someone closer, someone who had betrayed her? She couldn't afford to get caught slipping.

As she sipped her champagne, her eyes scanned the room, looking for anything out of place. That's when she saw him.

Jake. The man who once held the key to her future... or so he thought. The man who thought he could control her. He'd been in the picture for months now, ever since she'd played the long con, worming her way into his life, his trust.

She tilted her head slightly, the corners of her lips curling into that signature smile—the one that always seemed to make men believe she was just a pretty face. But she was so much more than that.

Dr. Monique Rodgers

Jake walked towards her, his eyes bright with excitement. He was oblivious to everything that was really going on. Still, he was useful—**for now.**

"You look stunning, Takina," he said, sitting down beside her. His voice was smooth, but Takina could hear the edge of desperation there. Men always got desperate when they thought they were close to winning her over.

"Thanks, Jake," she replied with a soft laugh, her fingers tracing the rim of her glass. She could feel his eyes on her, and the way his breath hitched when she glanced at him just right.

Dr. Monique Rodgers

"I've been thinking about us," Jake said, leaning forward, "about what comes next."

Takina raised an eyebrow. **What comes next?** She already knew what was coming next. Men like Jake always thought they had her figured out, but they never did. She had him where she wanted him.

"I think it's time for us to make it official," he said, a smug look crossing his face. "Let's go public. You and me—together. This could be big, Takina. I've got connections, you've got the brains. We'd be unstoppable."

Takina fought the urge to roll her eyes. **Unstoppable?** He had no idea. She already had plans—plans that didn't involve him. Jake was just a stepping stone in her bigger scheme, a part of her web that was about to be spun tight.

She leaned in close, lowering her voice to a near whisper. "Jake... you're sweet. You really are. But I think you're getting ahead of yourself."

He blinked, clearly thrown off guard. Takina had always been able to make men believe in something that didn't exist, and it was one of the things she was best at. **Emotional manipulation.**

"You're saying no?" Jake asked, his face dropping.

Takina leaned back, her gaze cold. "No, I'm saying you've already said too much. You've made it all about you, when it should have been about us. We were a team, Jake. But you got greedy. You wanted more than I was willing to give, and now you're out of your depth."

She watched his expression shift from confusion to anger, and she could practically hear the wheels turning in his head. He was going to try to turn this around, just like every other man who thought he could handle her.

But Takina was done playing his game.

"Get out," she said, her tone icy.

Jake's jaw clenched, but he stood up, his eyes full of fury. "You'll regret this, Takina. You'll see."

Takina didn't flinch. She had heard those words more times than she cared to count. Jake would be no different. She had already won this round.

As he stormed off, Takina took a deep breath. The night was far from over. She had her own battles to fight, but she wasn't about to let anyone—especially not Jake—get in her way.

Her phone buzzed again. Another text, from the same unknown number:

"You won't escape this, Takina. The truth always comes out."

Takina's lips twisted into a smile as she deleted the message. She didn't fear the truth. In fact, she was **the**

truth. And the longer they chased her, the more she thrived.

In the end, no one could catch the **Black Widow**.

Chapter 12:

The Final Web

Takina sat in the shadows of her penthouse, watching the city skyline from her floor-to-ceiling windows. It was a different kind of night—darker, heavier, like something was about to break. Her mind was racing, ticking through every single move, every plan she'd laid out so meticulously. She had done it all. Played them all. And now it was time to finish it.

The phone buzzed on the table beside her, cutting through the silence. Her eyes didn't even flicker toward it at first. She already knew what it would say. The same message she'd been receiving for days.

Dr. Monique Rodgers

"We know you're behind it all. You're not untouchable, Takina. We'll find you."

Takina smirked, her fingers brushing the sleek screen of her phone as she deleted the message. "Try me," she muttered under her breath.

She had played this game too long, too well, to let it slip now. The last threads of her carefully constructed web were about to snap. She had set the trap. She'd watched as her enemies stumbled into it. Now, it was time to watch them fall.

A soft knock at the door broke her concentration. She didn't even need to ask who it was.

"Come in, Jake," she said, her voice smooth, but with an edge that was hard to ignore. She was done being nice to him. Done pretending.

Jake stepped into the room, his face a mix of confusion and disbelief. His suit was impeccable, but his eyes—those eyes—betrayed him. He was nervous.

"Takina," he started, his voice shaking just a little, "we need to talk. This whole thing's getting out of hand."

She raised an eyebrow. "You came here to talk? After everything you've done?" She let the words hang in the air for a moment. "Jake, you're not the one in control here. You never were."

He tried to move closer, but she held up a hand, signaling him to stop. "Don't come any closer," she warned.

Jake stopped in his tracks, clearly thrown by the coldness in her voice. "You can't just—"

Takina stood up slowly, eyes locked on him. "I already have. You should've known when to back off. But no, you had to dig deeper, didn't you? You had to think you could handle the Black Widow."

His lips pressed together, and for a split second, she saw the fear. It was real. She could almost taste it in the air.

"You think you've got it all figured out, huh?" he finally spat, trying to hold on to some shred of pride. "But this isn't over, Takina. You've messed with the wrong people."

She took a step closer, her heels clicking against the marble floor, the sound echoing through the empty room. "Don't you get it? It's already over. And I'm the one who's won."

He scoffed. "You're playing a dangerous game."

She tilted her head, a smirk curling at the corners of her mouth. "You should've read the fine print, Jake. I don't play games. I play for keeps."

Dr. Monique Rodgers

The air between them crackled with tension, but Takina was unfazed. She had planned for this moment, for every possible scenario. She wasn't going to be intimidated by Jake—or anyone else.

"You think you can just disappear? Walk away from all of this?" Jake asked, voice rising with frustration. "You're delusional."

She moved toward the door, flipping off the lights. "Jake, it's time to go. And I suggest you leave before I make you."

Before he could respond, she was out the door, moving with the grace and purpose of a predator closing in on her prey. She didn't need to hear his protests anymore. She knew what she had to do.

Outside, the night air felt sharp, crisp with the weight of inevitability. Takina slid into her sleek black car, the engine purring to life as she sped off into the streets. The city lights blurred in the rearview mirror, fading into the distance like the last remnants of a dream.

She wasn't going to run. Not anymore. Not from anyone.

Her phone buzzed again. This time, she didn't hesitate. She answered the call.

"Takina." The voice on the other end was cold, familiar. Victor Cruz. He had finally found her. But what he didn't know was that she was ready.

"I told you, I'd make you regret this," Victor's voice rasped, full of arrogance.

Takina's lips parted into a slow smile. "Victor, I don't regret a thing. And you're about to see why."

She clicked the phone off without another word, her heart beating in sync with the pounding bass of the music in her car. She had the upper hand. She always had.

Minutes later, Takina arrived at the safe house, a discreet building tucked away from prying eyes. Inside, she took a deep breath, steadying herself for what was coming next. There would be no turning back.

As she moved into the back room, she saw her final piece in place—a thick envelope, filled with everything she needed to make her next move.

The phone buzzed once more, but this time it wasn't a warning. This time, it was an invitation.

"You think you've won, but we're coming for you."

Takina chuckled darkly, shaking her head. "No, Victor. You're not coming for me. You're already too late."

With a single swipe of her hand, she shredded the envelope, scattering the contents across the room—plans, secrets, lies, and betrayal.

They had underestimated her. And now they'd pay the price.

Dr. Monique Rodgers

She was the Black Widow. And this web she'd spun? It

was unbreakable.

About the Author

Dr. Monique Rodgers is an international bestselling author, CEO, visionary, and master business coach whose extraordinary career spans a multitude of disciplines. A certified vegan health coach, motivational speaker, entrepreneur, educator, and Mary Kay independent advanced color & skin care consultant, Dr. Rodgers is widely recognized as a literary genius and notable writing coach. She is the founder and serial entrepreneur behind several successful ventures, and her remarkable work continues to inspire and impact the lives of countless individuals worldwide.

Throughout her career, Dr. Rodgers has authored an impressive 155 books, including renowned titles such as *Hello! My Name is Millennial, Picking Up the Pieces, The Mystical Land of Twinville, Falling in Love with Jesus, Accelerate, Overcoming Writer's Block, Just Breathe, Called to Intercede Volumes 1-14,* and *I Am Black History,* to name just a few. Additionally, she has contributed as a co-author in collaborations like *Jumpstart Your Mind, Speak Up: We Deserve to Be Heard, Finding Joy in the Journey Volume 2,* and *Let the Kingdompreneurs Speak.*

Dr. Rodgers' exceptional work has earned her numerous

accolades and recognition, including the prestigious Presidential Lifetime Achievement Award in 2023. She is also a proud member of the KDP Scholars & Honor Society, underscoring her standing as a distinguished leader in the literary world. Dr. Rodgers has graced prominent media platforms such as *Rachel Speaks Radio Program*, *The Love Walk Podcast*, *The Glory Network*, *God's Glory Radio Show*, *The Miracle Zone*, *The Healing Zone*, *The Joyce Kiwani Adams Show*, and many others, where she shares her wisdom and insights with global audiences.

Her presence has been felt on multiple platforms, and she has served as a TV host for WATCTV. Her work has been featured in *Heart and Soul Magazine*, *My Story the Magazine*, and Kish Magazine's *Top 20 Authors of 2021*.

She has also been honored with inclusion in *Marquis Who's Who in America 2021-2022*. Beyond her literary endeavors, Dr. Rodgers is dedicated to volunteerism, having served on the executive team of *Lady Deliverers Arise*, as a board member for *Aniyah Space*, and as a member of the *I Am My Sister* organization.

A certified master business coach and health advocate, Dr. Rodgers has played key leadership roles in both the business and ministry sectors. She currently serves as an Awakening Prayer Hub leader in Raleigh, under the tutelage of Apostle Jennifer LeClaire, and as an ambassador for Kingdom Sniper Institute, mentored by Evangelist Latrice Ryan. Dr. Rodgers' academic credentials include an undergraduate degree from Oral Roberts University, a Master of Science degree, and a doctorate in global leadership from Colorado Technical

University. She has also studied at The Black Business School online.

Looking ahead, Dr. Rodgers remains committed to expanding her expertise and serving others through ministry. Her vision includes helping over one hundred authors complete and publish their books, training intercessors to deepen their relationship with God, and equipping marketplace prophets and leaders for success. Driven by her passion for empowering others, Dr. Rodgers continues to influence and inspire, using her voice and platform to bring about lasting change and positive transformation in the lives of many.

To stay connected with Dr. Monique Rodgers

<u>Contact information:</u>
www.getwriteoncoaching.com
www.meetdrmonique.com
Facebook: www.facebook.com/moniquerodgers2
Instagram: @drroyalty7
Twitter: @DrMonique7
LinkedIn: Dr. Monique Rodgers
YouTube: Dr. Monique Rodgers
Clubhouse: @DrMonique7
Email: calledtointerecede@gmail.com

10 upcoming crime thrillers by Dr. Monique Rodgers, set to be released in 2025:

1. **The Silent Betrayal** A gripping tale of a successful businesswoman who learns that the price of success comes with dangerous betrayals lurking in the shadows. Trust no one.

2. **The Shadows We Keep** When a detective uncovers a series of unsolved cold cases, he becomes entangled in a deadly game with someone who has a long-buried past and secrets worth killing for.

3. **Behind Closed Doors** A heart-pounding psychological thriller about a seemingly perfect family, whose dark secrets threaten to destroy them all, as a mysterious figure emerges from the shadows to tear them apart.

4. **Crimson Lies** A mysterious death in a wealthy family unveils a trail of lies, jealousy, and deception. The killer is closer than anyone realizes, and the truth is more shocking than anyone could imagine.

5. **The Stolen Identity** A woman's life is turned upside down when she discovers her identity has been stolen by a dangerous criminal mastermind, and now she must race against time to reclaim everything she's lost.

6. **Whispers in the Dark** A detective hunting for answers to a string of disappearances realizes the key to solving the case may lie in a series of cryptic messages left by the victims themselves.

7. **The Price of Revenge** After a brutal betrayal, an innocent man is sent to prison for a crime he didn't commit. Once free, he seeks vengeance against the powerful forces that ruined his life—but revenge comes with its own price.

8. **The Final Witness** The last surviving witness to a horrific crime becomes the target of those who want to ensure the truth never comes to light. It's a race to the finish as he fights to stay alive and expose the conspiracies at play.

9. **Broken Trust** An investigator seeking justice for a murdered socialite unravels a web of deceit involving everyone she knew. What was thought to be a simple case turns into a deadly game of

cat and mouse.

10. **The Deadly Agenda** In this high-stakes thriller, a group of ruthless criminals with hidden agendas begins to target key figures in a major city. A lone, troubled detective must navigate through corruption and murder to stop them before it's too late.